Catching the Moon

Written by Mal Peet and Elspeth Graham
Illustrated by Xiao Xin

D0785705

It was time to go to bed.
Hal had a tantrum.
He shouted and yelled.
He stamped his feet.

"What is the matter?" asked the Queen.
"What do you want?" asked the King.
"I want the moon!" yelled Hal.

"You shall have the moon," said the Queen.
The King called for the servants.
"You must go and catch the moon," he said.

4

The servants were called Grim and Crumb.
Grim was tall and thin.
Crumb was short and fat.
They set off to catch the moon.

The servants went out into the garden.
The moon was high up in the sky.
"There it is," said Grim.
"How shall we catch it?" asked Crumb.

"I have a plan," said Crumb.
"We need a ladder, a net, a big hook
and some string."

The servants put the ladder by the tree.
But they could not catch the moon.
"I have a plan," said Crumb.

8

The servants went up to the top of the tower. But they could not reach the moon.

9

The servants saw the moon in the pond.
"I will catch it in my net," said Crumb.
"Then I will tie it up with string," said Grim.

Splash!

Crumb and Grim fell in the pond.
The moon would not stay still.
It wiggled and wobbled.
They could not catch the moon.

Grim and Crumb were wet and cross.
They could not catch the moon.
They went to tell the King and Queen.

The King and Queen were very happy.
The moon was right outside the window!
"Here is the moon! You caught it," they cried.
But little Hal was fast asleep.

A story map

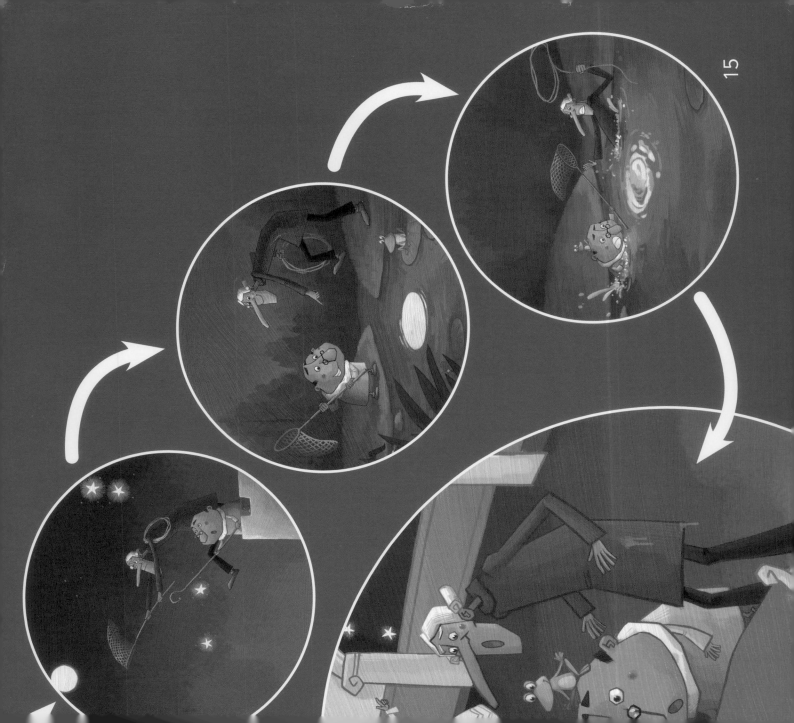

 Ideas for reading

Written by Clare Dowdall PhD
Lecturer and Primary Literacy Consultant

Learning objectives: retell stories, ordering events using story language; recognise automatically an increasing number of familiar high frequency words; apply phonic knowledge and skills as the prime approach to reading unfamiliar words that are not completely decodable; identify the main events and characters in stories and find specific information in simple texts

Curriculum links: Art and Design: Mother Nature; Science: Earth, Sun and Moon

Focus phonemes: ch, al, ow, au, -y

Fast words: was, to, go, he, what, do, said, we, have, some, put, by, could, very

Word count: 269

Getting started

- Introduce the focus phonemes and practise saying them aloud in isolation and within words, e.g. *al* (Hal), *ow* (how, tower), *au* (caught), *-y* (happy).

- Dwell on the *ow* phoneme. Remind children of the other phoneme made by these letters, e.g. grow, know.

- Read the title and blurb with the children. Dwell on the word *catching*. Revise the *ch* phoneme, and suggest other words that contain the *ch* phoneme.

- Revise the fast words *put, could, very* using flash cards.

Reading and responding

- Look at pp2–3 together. Model using phonic knowledge to tackle unfamiliar words, e.g. *t-a-n-t-r-u-m*.

- Model how to read pp2–3 aloud with expression, using appropriate voices for each character.

- Ask children to look at the words *wiggled* and *wobbled* on p11. Ask children to explain how they will read these words and what is special about them, e.g. *-ed* ending.

- Ask children to read the rest of the book aloud. Ask them to notice new and tricky words and to use phonics to read them.